MW00979659

Autograph Page

Autograph Page

This book is dedicated to
the Folds of Honor Foundation
as well as the men, women and families who make
the ultimate sacrifice to ensure our freedom.
To learn more about Folds of Honor Foundation,
visit www.FoldsofHonor.org.

SCOOTER PINES PUBLISHING
An imprint of Scooter Pines Holdings, LLC
P.O. Box 5365, Virginia Beach, Virginia 23471

Scooter Pines Publishing is a subsidiary of Scooter Pines Holdings, LLC.
Book design by Scott McLaughlin Fuller
The text for this book is set in Calisto MT.
The illustrations for this book are rendered in colored pencils.

Library of Congress Cataloging-in-Publication Data is available.

Bogey Ballton's Night Before Christmas / by Dottie Pepper & Scott Fuller;
illustrated by Kenneth Templeton

SUMMARY: On Christmas Eve, Bogey startles Santa Ball and learns the
true meaning of Christmas.

ISBN 13: 978-0-9850141-2-4

Printed in The United States of America

A portion of the proceeds from each book sold will go
to help support the Folds of Honor Foundation.

Bogey Ballton's Night Before Christmas

Based on
Clement C. Moore's
"A Visit from Saint Nicholas"

By Dottie Pepper & Scott Fuller
Illustrated by Kenneth Templeton

Scooter Pines Publishing
USA

'Twas the night

before Christmas, when all through the course
The 'Better Be Sleeping' rule was strictly in force.
Too anxious to sleep, Bogey spun in despair,
Knowing the outcome and what wouldn't be there.

His best friends were nestled all snug in their beds,
While visions of hole-n-ones danced in their heads;
And Ma Ballton with earplugs and Pa snoring loud,
Bogey's tossing and turning wasn't allowed.

"If I don't fall asleep, if I stay wide awake,
Santa Ball won't come see me, help me for Pete's sake!"
When outside his window arose such a clatter,
He sprang to his feet to see what was the matter.

The moon reflecting off the new-fallen snow,
Gave the shine of mid-day to Duffer's Den below,
When what to his panicking eyes should appear,
But a tiny golf cart pulled by eight balls of cheer,

With a little old driver so lively and round,
He knew in a moment whom he had just found.
More rapid than tee shots his golf balls they came,
And he whistled, and shouted, and called them by name:

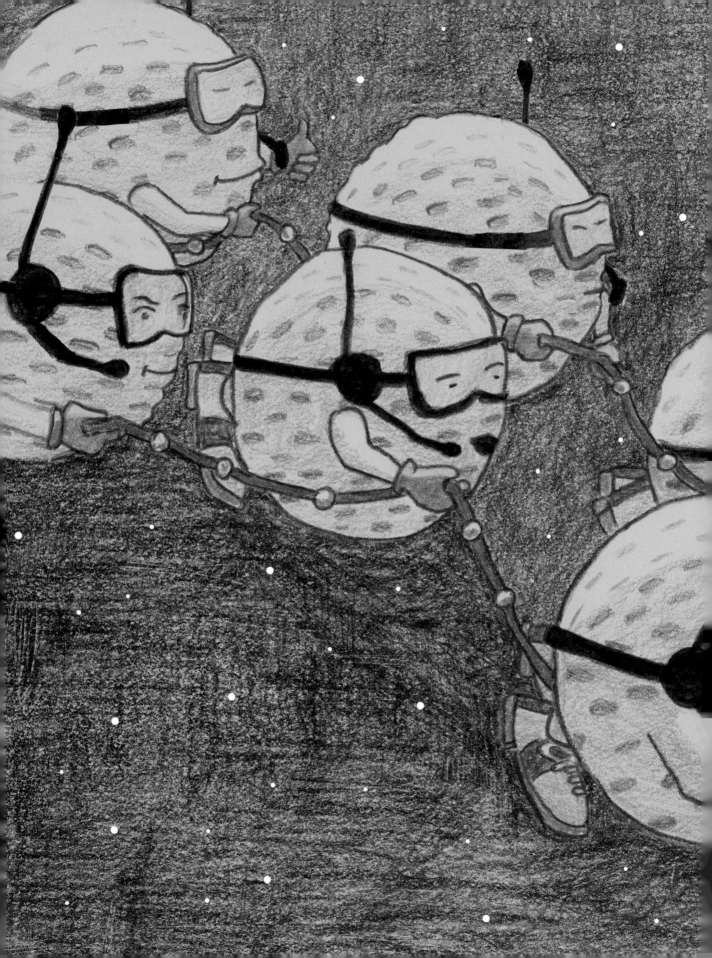

"Now, Duffer! Now, Putter! Now, Slicer and Chip-in!
On, Chopper! On, Divot! On, Birdie and Backspin!
To the top of the bunker! To the sand, do not fall!
Now bounce away! Bounce away! Bounce away ball!"

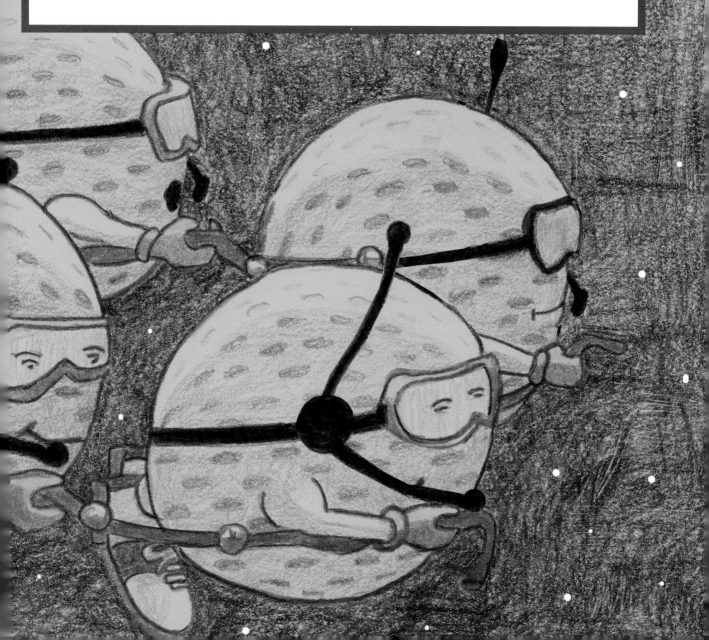

As golf balls that are struck before the practice range fly,
When they meet a lofty club, they bound for the sky;
So up to the shoe box roof top the balls flew,
With the golf cart full of toys, and Santa Ball too.

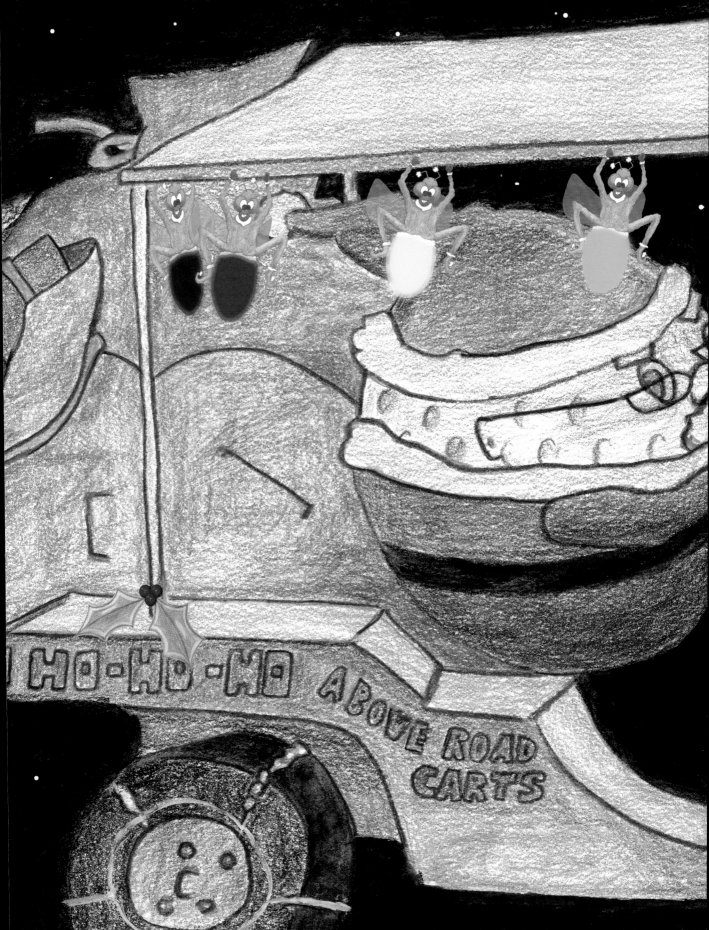

And then, in an instant, Bogey heard on the roof,
Four tires skidding to a stop with a poof.
As he drew in his head and was turning to see,
Down the chimney Santa Ball bounced, landing with glee.

He was dressed all in fleece, from his head to his toe,
And his clothes were all covered with ashes and snow.
A bundle of toys he then dropped with a wag,
And he looked like a caddy just opening his bag.

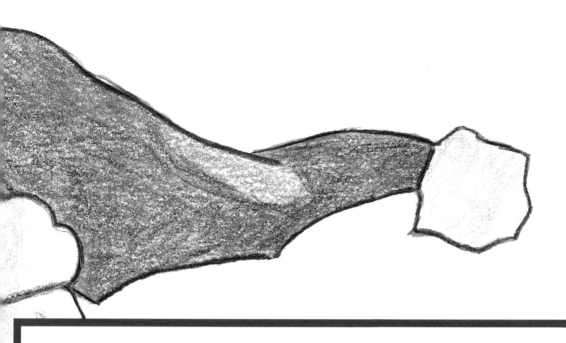

His eyes, how they twinkled! His dimples, very cute!
His cheeks were wind blown, his nose red from the commute!
His funny small mouth twisted up in a smile,
And his long white beard had not been trimmed in a while.

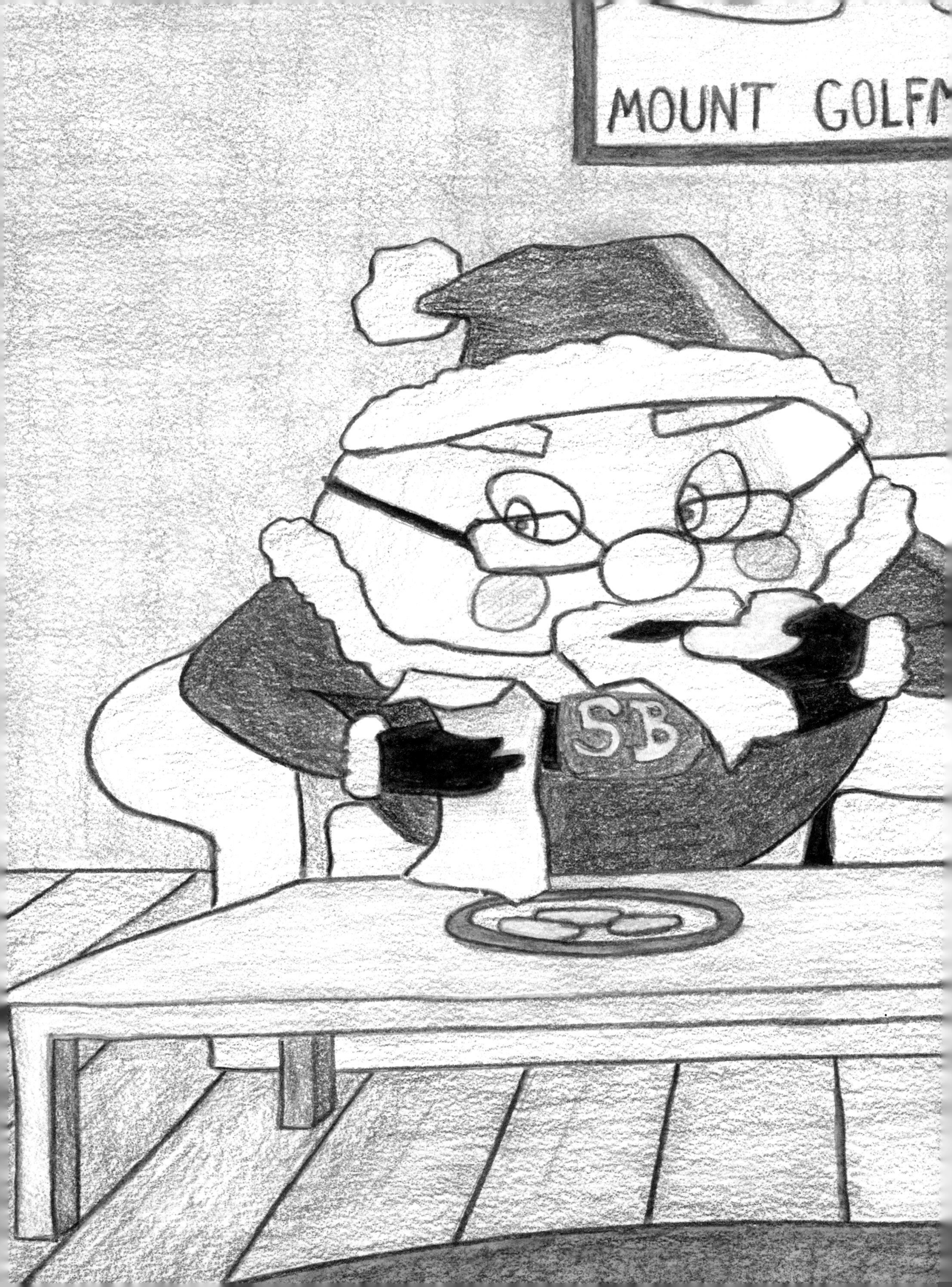
MOUNT GOLF
SB

The hat on his head kept him warm through the flight,
And the glove on his hand gripped a cookie real tight.
Enjoying every mouthful and reading his note,
He never heard Bogey 'til he cleared out his throat!

Santa Ball bounced up high, scared half out of his wits,
"You're not supposed to see me or I must call it quits!"
Bogey wobbled there before him pleading his case,
Explaining the truth and turning red in the face.

"That is all fine and dandy, my little round friend,
But a rule is a rule and that's how this will end."
Disappointed and sad, Bogey questioned the night,
"What's the point of Christmas with no presents in sight?"

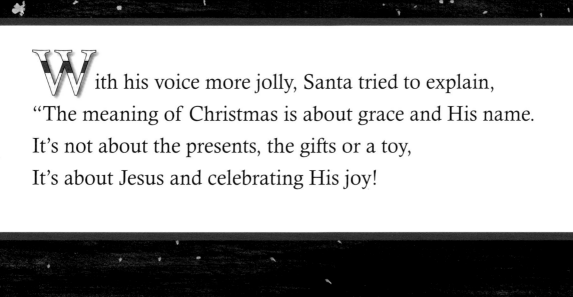

With his voice more jolly, Santa tried to explain,
"The meaning of Christmas is about grace and His name.
It's not about the presents, the gifts or a toy,
It's about Jesus and celebrating His joy!

So think of this eve, when you finally do rest,
Jesus our Savior was born, for this we are blessed!
The gifts remind us of His glory and love,
Remember His story, the true gift from above!"

CLICK!

With that being said, Santa's job was done now,
He pulled from his jacket 'the candy cane of wow'.
With its flash like lightning the cane he did click,
Bogey's memory of him had vanished real quick!

With a wink of Santa's eye, a nod of his head,
Bogey floated down the hall and back in his bed.
Exactly how it happened will never be clear,
But the true meaning of Christmas he now holds dear.

With no one around, Santa Ball went to work,
And filled all the stockings, then turned with a jerk.
And the snap of his fingers, the tap of his boot,
He rose up the chimney with the rest of his loot.

He sprang to his golf cart, to his team gave the sign,
Away they all flew like an airplane on time.
He exclaimed with joy as he continued his flight,

Merry Christmas to all,

and to Bogey,
a Good-Night!